First published in Great Britain in 2017 by Pat-a-Cake
This edition published 2019
Copyright © Hodder & Stoughton Limited 2017. All rights reserved
Pat-a-Cake is a registered trade mark of Hodder & Stoughton Limited
ISBN: 978 1 52638 267 2 • 10 9 8 7 6 5 4 3 2 1
Pat-a-Cake, an imprint of Hachette Children's Group,
Part of Hodder & Stoughton Limited
Carmelite House, 50 Victoria Embankment, London EC4Y 0DZ
An Hachette UK Company
www.hachette.co.uk • www.hachettechildrens.co.uk
Printed in China

My Very First Story Time

Cinderella

Retold by Rachel Elliot

Illustrated by Tim Budgen

pat a cake

Cinderella

stepmother

stepsisters

invitation

magic wand

Fairy
Godmother

mouse

pumpkin

rat

dress

clock

glass slipper

Prince

carriage

coachman

horses

ONCE UPON A TIME, there was a young girl called Cinderella. She lived with her mean stepmother and her two silly stepsisters. Cinderella did everything for her lazy family.

One day, an invitation arrived from the palace.

"Oh my, oh my, oh my!" trilled Cinderella's stepmother.
"There's to be a ball at the palace and we're invited!"
The silly stepsisters screamed in delight.
"Does that mean I can go, too?" asked Cinderella, wide-eyed.
"YOU?" cackled her stepmother. "Of course not!"

Cinderella worked hard to help her stepsisters look their best. Late into the night, she sewed stitch upon tiny stitch with delicate silken thread. The gowns glittered with sequins and rustled with rich satin petticoats.

The silly stepsisters primped and preened and polished and cleaned until, at last, they were ready for the ball.

When they had gone, tiny tears tumbled down Cinderella's cheeks.
"Oh, I do wish I could go to the ball," she cried.
Suddenly, the room went dark and there was a flash of light.

Cinderella looked up to see a glittering fairy hovering close by. "I am your Fairy Godmother," she said. "And you shall go to the ball."

Cinderella gasped, as a flash of the fairy's wand turned a pumpkin into a carriage of gold, some squeaking mice into prancing horses and a big old rat into a coachman.

Smiling at Cinderella, she said, "Well, you can't go dressed like that!" With a sparkling swoosh, Cinderella's ragged clothes became a glittering dress, while slippers of glass shimmered on her feet.

"Am I dreaming?" whispered Cinderella.

"It's magic," explained her Fairy Godmother.

"But my spell will stop as the clock strikes midnight."

When Cinderella arrived at the palace, everyone gasped in wonder. Their whispers floated on the breeze until they reached the Prince himself. He followed the murmuring voices into the courtyard.

When Cinderella stepped from the golden carriage, the Prince's heart skipped a beat. She was the most beautiful girl he had ever seen.

Inside the palace ballroom, glamorous guests watched
as the Prince and Cinderella began to dance.
Round and round they spun, talking and twirling, laughing
and whirling as the music played and time tick-tocked by.

After what seemed like only a few minutes to Cinderella, the clock began to strike midnight, and she remembered her Fairy Godmother's warning.

As she ran from the palace, Cinderella felt the magic disappear
with every step. The Prince rushed after her, but she was gone.
All that remained was a glass slipper, glittering in the moonlight.
"I MUST find the girl whose foot fits this shoe," cried the Prince.

The next day, the Prince took the glass slipper to every home in his kingdom. He visited castles and cottages. He tried it upon the feet of duchesses and dairymaids.

But none could squeeze her foot into the delicate slipper.

At last, the Prince visited the house where Cinderella lived.
The slipper was too tiny for her stepmother and silly stepsisters.
"Does anyone else live here?" asked the Prince, looking around
the untidy house.

At that moment, Cinderella came into the room. Her clothes were rags, but the Prince knew who she was at once. The glass slipper fitted her delicate foot perfectly.

Her stepsisters were amazed . . . and very annoyed.
"Will you marry me?" asked the handsome Prince.
"I will," answered Cinderella.

And they lived happily ever after.

YOU SHALL GO TO THE BALL!

What would you wear to the ball?

Tiaras

Pick your favourites . . .

With
REAL
jewels!

Gowns

Feel like a princess in
our glorious gowns.

Be ready for that
royal invitation!

Footwear

Dance all night in our shimmering shoes.

Large sizes available.

Fans

All shoes come with our **No Nasty Niffs**™ guarantee!

Keep your cool at the ball!

And something for gentlemen . . .

Socks

Buy one sock, get second FREE!

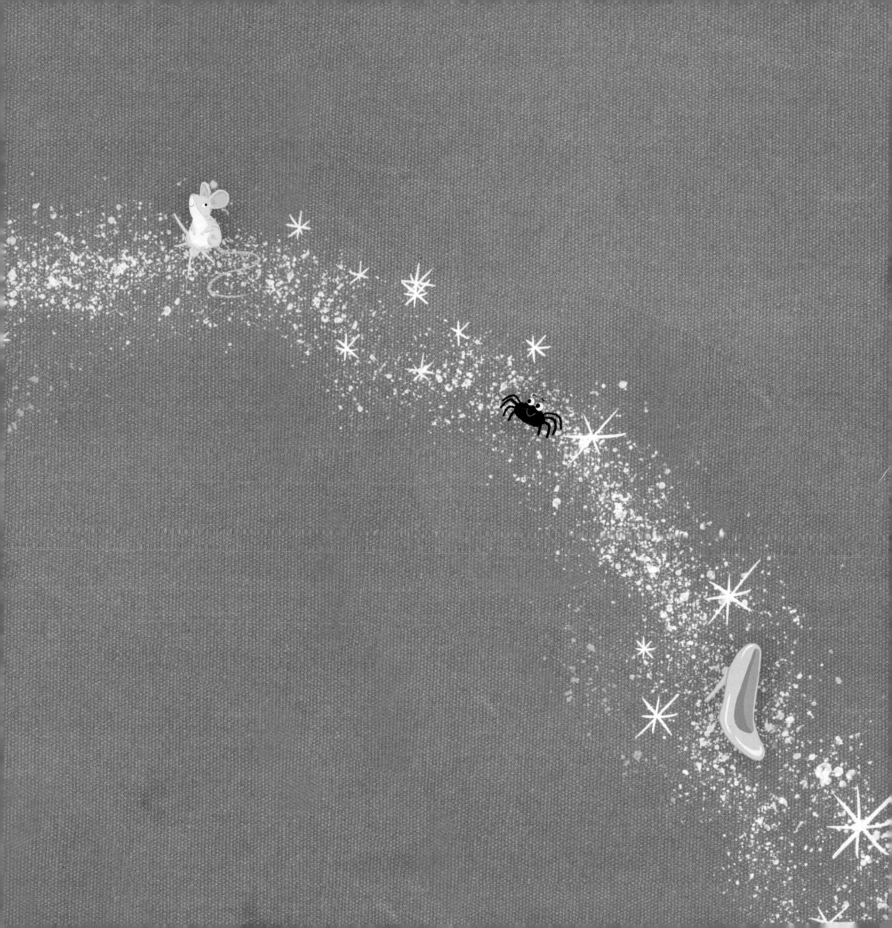